Summer Treasure

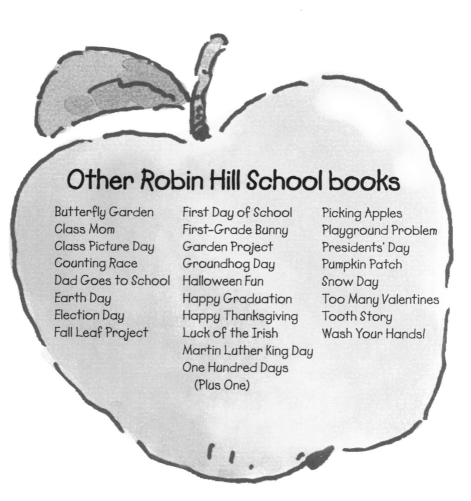

Other Robin Hill School books

Robin Hill School

Summer Treasure

written by Margaret McNamara
illustrated by Mike Gordon

Ready-to-Read

Simon Spotlight
New York   London   Toronto   Sydney   New Delhi

For teachers everywhere—M. M.

Simon Spotlight
An imprint of Simon & Schuster Children's Publishing Division
1230 Avenue of the Americas, New York, NY 10020
Text copyright © 2012 by Margaret McNamara
Illustrations copyright © 2012 by Mike Gordon
For information about special discounts for bulk purchases, please contact
Simon & Schuster Special Sales at 1-866-506-1949 or business@simonandschuster.com.
The Simon & Schuster Speakers Bureau can bring authors to your live event. For more
information or to book an event contact the Simon & Schuster Speakers Bureau at
1-866-248-3049 or visit our website at www.simonspeakers.com.
Manufactured in the United States 0312 LAK
First Edition
2 4 6 8 10 9 7 5 3 1
Library of Congress Cataloging-in-Publication Data
McNamara, Margaret.
Summer treasure / by Margaret McNamara ; illustrated by Mike Gordon. – 1st ed.
p. cm. – (Robin Hill School) (Ready-to-read)
Summary: When Hannah goes to the beach with her mother, she is shocked
to find her first-grade teacher, Mrs. Connor, lying there in a bathing suit as
if she were an ordinary person.
ISBN 978-1-4424-3645-9 (pbk. : alk. paper) – ISBN 978-1-4424-3646-6 (hardcover : alk.
paper) – ISBN 978-1-4424-3647-3 (e-book)
[1. Teachers–Fiction. 2. Beaches–Fiction.] I. Gordon, Mike, 1948 Mar. 16- ill. II. Title.
PZ7.M47879343Sum 2012   [E]–dc23   2011027462

School was over.

Hannah was on vacation.

One afternoon,
Hannah went to the beach
with her mom.

Hannah brought a shovel
and a pail.

"I will look for treasure!"
Hannah told her mom.

Before Hannah found
the perfect spot for digging,
she found something else.
She found . . .

MRS. CONNOR!

Hannah could not believe
her eyes.

Mrs. Connor was here!

At the beach!

She was wearing
a swimsuit!
She had sunglasses!
And her hair was not
in a ponytail!

"Hello, Hannah,"
said Mrs. Connor.
She was acting as if
nothing was wrong.
"Mrs. Connor!" said
Hannah.

"What are you doing here?"

"I am at the beach,"
said Mrs. Connor, "with
my husband."

Mrs. Connor had a husband!

"You should be at school!"
said Hannah.
"I am not at school
all the time,"
said Mrs. Connor.

"Sometimes I have vacation, just like you."
Now Hannah could not believe her ears.

"I thought teachers
lived at school all year,"
said Hannah.

"I thought they had dinner together . . .

. . . then they watched
a little TV . . .

. . . then they put on
their pajamas . . .

. . . and then they went to
sleep in bunk beds."

"No," said Mrs. Connor.
"Teachers do not live at
school all the time.

They go home
just like you do.
They have families
just like you do."

"My husband is swimming,"
said Mrs. Connor.
"Do you want to play
for a while?"

Hannah and Mrs. Connor
looked for shells.

They dipped into the water.

They dug for treasure,
but they did not find any.
Then they waved good-bye.

When Hannah got home,
her brother asked,
"Did you find any treasure
at the beach?"

Hannah looked into
her empty pail.
Hannah thought about
Mrs. Connor.
"Yes," said Hannah. "I did!"